MW00906437

The Secret Garden Coloring Book

Frances Hodgson Burnett

Adapted by Brian Doherty
Illustrated by Thea Kliros

Dover Publications, Inc.
New York

Copyright

Copyright © 1993 by Dover Publications, Inc.
All rights reserved under Pan American and International Copyright Conventions.

Published in Canada by General Publishing Company, Ltd., 30 Lesmill Road, Don Mills, Toronto, Ontario.

Bibliographical Note

The Secret Garden Coloring Book is a new work, first published by Dover Publications, Inc., in 1993. The text is a new abridgement of the work originally published by William Heinemann, London, in 1911.

DOVER *Pictorial Archive* SERIES

This book belongs to the Dover Pictorial Archive Series. You may use the designs and illustrations for graphics and crafts applications, free and without special permission, provided that you include no more than four in the same publication or project. (For permission for additional use, please write to Dover Publications, Inc., 31 East 2nd Street, Mineola, N.Y. 11501.)

However, republication or reproduction of any illustration by any other graphic service whether it be in a book or in any other design resource is strictly prohibited.

International Standard Book Number: 0-486-27680-5

Manufactured in the United States of America
Dover Publications, Inc., 31 East 2nd Street, Mineola, N.Y. 11501

When Mary Lennox was sent to Misselthwaite Manor to live with her uncle, everybody said she was the most disagreeable-looking child ever seen. She had a little thin face and a little thin body, yellow hair and a sour expression.

Her parents were English and were living in India when Mary was born. Her mother had not wanted a girl and so Mary was kept out of sight, in the care of servants who always let her have her way. Because of this, Mary became very spoiled, and by the age of six she was as demanding and selfish a little girl as ever lived.

One day, all that changed. An outbreak of disease struck the Lennoxes' part of India. Most of the servants died and the household fell into chaos. In the confusion Mary hid herself away in the nursery, forgotten by a world that didn't care about her and that she didn't care about. After waiting and sleeping for hours and hours she finally heard footsteps and men's voices enter the house.

"What desolation!" she heard a voice say. "That pretty woman! I heard there was a child, though no one ever saw her."

Mary stood frowning, cross and ugly, when they opened the door to the nursery. She was getting hungry and feeling miserably neglected. The officers were very surprised to find her there. Mary, however, was upset and demanded to know why no one had come to her.

"There is nobody left to come," she was told.

And so it was that Mary came to realize that her parents had died in the night and the surviving servants had fled. She had never really known her parents, except from a distance, so she was not really upset that they had gone. She only thought of herself and hoped that she would be going to stay with nice people who would give her her own way.

After staying a while with a poor English clergyman's family, where she was as unpleasant as ever, Mary was sent by boat to England to stay with her uncle, Mr. Archibald Craven, at Misselthwaite Manor. She was met in London by Mr. Craven's housekeeper, Mrs. Medlock, a stout woman with very red cheeks and sharp black eyes. She was wearing a purple dress and a black bonnet with purple velvet flowers that shook when she moved her head. Mary did not like her and did nothing to disguise the fact. Mrs. Medlock returned the favor.

"My word! she's a plain little thing!" she said. "And we'd heard that her mother was a beauty."

Each thought the other the most disagreeable person she had ever met. Mrs. Medlock, however, had been instructed to bring Mary to Yorkshire and she was not going to put up with any nonsense from the child. On the train, Mrs. Medlock described the house they were going to.

"The house is six hundred years old and there's near a hundred rooms. And there's a big park round it and gardens and trees with branches trailing to the ground."

Mary pretended not to be interested, in her disagreeable way, but she was.

"Don't you care?" Mrs. Medlock asked. "One thing's sure, *he's*," meaning Mr. Craven, "not going to trouble himself about you. He never troubles himself about no one. He's got a crooked back. That set him wrong. He was a sour young man and got no good of his money and place till he was married."

Mary seemed more interested and Mrs. Medlock went on to tell how Mr. Craven and his wife loved each other very much but that the wife had died. All of a sudden Mary felt sorry for Mr. Craven.

"You probably won't see him," said Mrs. Medlock. "You'll have to look after yourself. But when you're in the house don't go poking about. Mr. Craven won't have it."

"I shall not want to," said sour little Mary; and she no longer felt sorry for Mr. Archibald Craven. And she watched the rain through the train window until she fell asleep.

It was quite dark when she awakened again. The train had stopped at a station and Mrs. Medlock was shaking her.

"You have had a sleep!" she said. "It's time to open your eyes! We're at Thwaite Station and we've got a long drive before us."

A brougham stood on the road before the little outside platform. Mary saw that it was a smart little carriage and that it was a smart footman who helped her in, his long waterproof coat and the waterproof covering of his hat dripping with rain.

On and on they drove through the darkness. The road went up and down, and several times the carriage passed over a little bridge beneath which water rushed very fast with a great deal of noise. Mary felt as if the drive would never come to an end and that the wide, bleak moor was a wide expanse of black ocean through which she was passing on a strip of dry land.

Eventually they stopped before an immensely long but lowbuilt house that seemed to ramble round a stone court. At first Mary thought that there were no lights at all in the windows, but as she got out of the carriage she saw that one room in a corner upstairs showed a dull glow.

A neat, thin old man stood near the manservant who opened the door for them.

"You are to take her to her room," he said in a husky voice. "He doesn't want to see her. He's going to London in the morning."

And so Mary Lennox was led up staircases and through corridors, until a door opened in a wall and she found herself in a room with a fire in it and a supper on a table.

Mrs. Medlock said unceremoniously:

"Well, here you are! This room and the next are where you'll live—and you must keep to them. Don't you forget that!"

It was in this way Mistress Mary arrived at Misselthwaite Manor and she had perhaps never felt quite so contrary in all her life.

When she opened her eyes in the morning it was because a young housemaid had come into her room to light the fire and was kneeling on the hearth-rug taking out the cinders noisily.

"Are you going to be my servant?" Mary asked.

"I'm Mrs. Medlock's servant," she said stoutly. "An' she's Mrs. Craven's—but I'm to do the housemaid's work up here an' wait on you a bit. But you won't need much waitin' on."

If Mary Lennox had been a child who was ready to be amused she would perhaps have laughed at Martha's readiness to talk, but Mary only listened to her coldly. But gradually, as the girl rattled on in her good-tempered way, Mary began to notice what she was saying.

"There's twelve of us an' my father only gets sixteen shilling a week. Our Dickon, he's twelve years old and he's got a young pony he calls his own. He found it on th' moor with its mother when it was a little one an' he began to make friends with it an' give it bits o' bread an' young grass. Dickon's a kind lad an' animals likes him. You'll have to learn to play like other children does. Our Dickon goes off on th' moor by himself an' plays for hours. That's how he made friends with the pony."

It was really this mention of Dickon that made Mary decide to go out, though she was not aware of it.

"If tha' goes round that way tha'll come to th' gardens," Martha said, pointing to a gate in a wall of shrubbery. "One of th' gardens is locked up. No one has been in it for ten years."

"Why?" asked Mary in spite of herself. Here was another locked door added to the hundred in the strange house.

"Mr. Craven had it shut when his wife died so sudden. He won't let no one go inside. It was her garden. He locked th' door an' dug a hole and buried th' key."

Mary turned down the walk which led to the door in the shrubbery. When she had passed through it she found herself in great gardens, with wide lawns and winding walks. There were flower-beds, and evergreens clipped into strange shapes, and a pool

with an old gray fountain. But the flower-beds were bare and wintry
and the fountain was not playing. At the end of the path she was on
there seemed to be a long wall, with ivy growing over it. She found
that there was a green door in the ivy. She went through the door
and found one of several walled gardens that seemed to open into
one another. She came to a second green door. It opened quite easily
and she found herself in an orchard. There were walls all around
it—but no green door to be seen anywhere. Mary looked for it, and
noticed that the wall did not seem to end with the orchard but to
extend beyond it as if it enclosed a place on the other side.

She could see the tops of trees above the wall, and when she stood still she saw a bird with a bright red breast on the topmost branch of one of them, and suddenly he burst into his winter song—almost as if he had caught sight of her and was calling to her.

She listened to him and somehow his cheerful, friendly little whistle gave her a pleased feeling—the big closed house and big bare moor and big bare gardens had made her feel as if there was no one left in the world but herself. She was desolate, and the bright-breasted little robin brought a look into her sour little face that was almost a smile. She listened to him until he flew away. Perhaps he lived in the mysterious garden and knew all about it.

For days after that, Mary spent most of her time outdoors, on the moor, and looking at the wall surrounding what she was sure was the hidden garden.

"Why did Mr. Craven hate the garden?" Mary asked Martha one evening.

"It was Mrs. Craven's garden that she made when first they were married an' she just loved it, an' they used to 'tend the flowers themselves. An' none o' the gardeners was let to go in. Him and her used to go in an' shut th' door an' stay there hours an' hours, readin' and talkin'. An' she was just a bit of a girl an' there was an old tree with a branch bent like a seat on it. An' she used to sit there. But one day when she was sittin' there th' branch broke an' she fell on th' ground an' was hurt so bad that next day she died. Th' doctors thought he'd go out o' his mind an' die, too. That's why he hates it. No one's never gone in since, an' he won't let any one talk about it."

Mary did not ask any more questions. She looked at the red fire and listened to the wind "wutherin'." But as she was listening to the wind she began to listen to something else. It was a curious sound—it seemed almost as if a child were crying somewhere.

"Do you hear any one crying?" she said.

Martha suddenly looked confused.

"No," she answered. "It's the wind. It's got all sorts o' sounds."

"But listen," said Mary. "It's in the house—down one of those long corridors."

At that very moment a rushing draft blew open the door of the room they sat in with a crash and the crying sound was heard more plainly than ever.

"There!" said Mary. "I told you so! It is some one crying—and it isn't a grown-up person."

Martha ran and shut the door and turned the key.

"It was th' wind," said Martha stubbornly.

But something troubled and awkward in her manner made Mistress Mary stare very hard at her. She did not believe she was speaking the truth.

After a few days of rain in which she did not go outside, Mary went out to the gardens. She heard a chirp and a twitter, and when she looked at the bare flower-bed at her left side she saw her robin hopping about and pecking things out of the earth. She saw him hop over a small pile of freshly turned-up earth, and she saw something almost buried in the newly turned soil. It was something like a ring of rusty iron or brass and when the robin flew up into a tree nearby she put out her hand and picked the ring up. It was more than a ring, however; it was an old key that looked as if it had been long buried.

She looked at the key quite a long time. All she thought about the key was that if it was the key to the closed garden, and she could find out where the door was, she could perhaps open it and see what was inside the walls, and what had happened to the old rose-trees. Her inactive brain had been set to working, awakening her imagination. The fresh, strong, pure air from the moor had a great deal to do with it. Already she felt less "contrary," though she did not know why. She took the key in her pocket, and she made up her mind that she would always carry it with her when she went out, so that if she ever should find the hidden door she would be ready.

The next day, Martha gave Mary a present: a skipping-rope with a red and blue handle at each end.

"You just try it," urged Martha. "You can't skip a hundred at first, but if you practice you'll mount up. Put on tha' things and run an' skip out o' doors."

Mary felt a little awkward as she went out of the room. At first she had disliked Martha very much, but now she did not. Mary skipped round all the gardens and round the orchard, resting every few minutes. She stopped with a laugh of pleasure. There, lo and behold, was the robin swaying on a long branch of ivy. He greeted her with a chirp.

"You showed me where the key was yesterday," Mary said. "You ought to show me the door today!"

The robin flew from his swinging spray of ivy on to the top of the wall and he opened his beak and sang a loud, lovely trill, merely to show off. Mary had stepped close to the robin, and suddenly a gust of wind swung aside some loose ivy trails, and more suddenly still she jumped toward them and caught them in her hand. This she did because she had seen something under them—a round knob that had been covered by the leaves hanging over it. It was the knob of a door.

What was this under her hands that was square and made of iron that her fingers found a hole in? It was the lock of the door that had been closed ten years. She put her hand in her pocket and drew out the key. She put the key in and turned it. It took two hands to do it, but it did turn. She held back the swinging curtain of ivy and pushed back the door, which opened slowly—slowly.

Then she slipped through it, and shut it behind her, and stood with her back against it, looking about her and breathing quite fast with excitement, and wonder, and delight.

She was standing *inside* the secret garden. The high walls that shut it in were covered with the leafless stems of climbing roses which were so thick that they were matted together. All the ground was covered with grass of a wintry brown and out of it grew clumps of bushes which were surely rose-bushes if they were alive. Climbing roses had run all over the trees in the garden and swung down long tendrils which made light swaying curtains.

"How still it is!" she whispered. "How still!"

The robin flew down from his tree-top and hopped about or flew after her from one bush to another. He chirped a good deal and had a very busy air, as if he were showing her things. Everything was strange and silent and she seemed to be hundreds of miles away from any one, but somehow she did not feel lonely at all. All that troubled her was her wish that she knew whether all the roses were dead, or if perhaps some of them had lived and might put out leaves and buds as the weather got warmer. She thought she saw something sticking out of the black earth—some sharp little pale green points.

"Yes, they are tiny growing things and they *might* be crocuses or snowdrops or daffodils," she whispered. "It isn't a quite dead garden," she cried out softly to herself.

Mary searched about until she found a sharp piece of wood and knelt down and dug and weeded out the weeds and grass until she made nice little clear places around the green points. She worked in her garden until it was time to go to her midday dinner. Then she ran across the grass, pushed open the slow old door and slipped through it under the ivy. She had such red cheeks and such bright eyes and ate such a dinner that Martha was delighted.

"I wish the spring was here now," said Mary. "I want to see all the things that grow in England. I wish—I wish I had a little spade. How much would a spade cost—a little one?" Mary asked.

"Well," was Martha's reflective answer, "at Thwaite village I saw little garden sets with a spade an' a rake an' a fork all tied together for two shillings. They sell packages o' flower-seeds for a penny each, and our Dickon knows which is th' prettiest ones an' how to make 'em grow. He walks over to Thwaite many a day just for th' fun of it. If tha' could print we could write a letter to him an' ask him to go an' buy th' tools an' th' seeds at th' same time."

"How shall I get the things when Dickon buys them?"

"He'll bring 'em to you himself. He'll like to walk over this way."

"Oh!" exclaimed Mary, "then I shall see him! I never thought I should see Dickon."

The sun shone down for nearly a week on the secret garden. The Secret Garden was what Mary called it when she was thinking of it. She liked the name, and she liked still more the feeling that when its beautiful old walls shut her in no one knew where she was. It seemed almost like being shut out of the world in some fairy place.

There was a laurel-hedged walk which curved round the secret garden and ended at a gate which opened into a wood, in the park. She thought she would look into the wood and see if there were any rabbits hopping about. When she reached the gate she opened it and went through because she heard a low, peculiar whistling sound and wanted to find out what it was.

A boy was sitting under a tree, with his back against it, playing on a rough wooden pipe. He was a funny-looking boy about twelve.

Never had Mary seen such round and such blue eyes in any boy's face. On the trunk of the tree, a squirrel was clinging and watching him, and quite near him were two rabbits sitting up—it appeared as if they were all drawing near to listen to the strange little call his pipe seemed to make.

"Don't tha' move, he said. "It'd flight 'em. I'm Dickon. I know tha'rt Miss Mary."

"Did you get Martha's letter?" she asked.

He nodded his curly, rust-colored head. "That's why I come. I've got the garden tools. There's a little spade an' rake an' a fork an' hoe. Eh! they are good 'uns. An' th' woman in th' shop threw in a packet o' white poppy an' one o' blue larkspur when I bought th' other seeds."

They sat down and he took a little brown paper package out of his coat pocket. He untied the string and inside there were ever so many neater and smaller packages with a picture of a flower on each one.

"There's a lot o' mignonette an' poppies," he said. "Mignonette's th' sweetest-smellin' thing as grows." He told her what they looked like when they were flowers, he told her how to plant them, and watch them, and feed and water them.

"See here," he said suddenly, turning round to look at her. "I'll plant them for thee myself. Where is tha' garden?"

Mary did not know what to say, so for a whole minute she said nothing. And she felt as if she went red and then pale.

"Tha's got a bit o' garden, hasn't tha'?" Dickon said.

She held her hands tighter and turned her eyes toward him.

"Could you keep a secret, if I told you one? It's a great secret. I don't know what I should do if any one found it out. I believe I should die!" She said this last sentence quite fiercely.

"I'm keepin' secrets all th' time," he said. "If I couldn't keep

secrets from th' other lads, secrets about foxes' cubs, an' birds' nests, an' wild things' holes, there'd be naught safe on th' moor. Aye, I can keep secrets.''

Mistress Mary did not mean to put out her hand and clutch his sleeve but she did it.

''I've stolen a garden,'' she said very fast. ''It isn't mine. It isn't anybody's. Perhaps everything is dead in it already; I don't know. Nobody has any right to take it from me when I care about it and they don't. They're letting it die, all shut in by itself,'' she ended passionately, and she threw her arms over her face and burst out crying.

''Where is it?'' asked Dickon in a dropped voice.

''Come with me and I'll show you,'' she said.

She led him round the laurel path and to the walk where the ivy grew so thickly. He felt as if he were being led to look at some strange bird's nest and must move softly. When she stepped to the wall and lifted the hanging ivy he started. There was a door and they passed in together, and then Mary stood and waved her hand round defiantly.

''It's this,'' she said. ''It's a secret garden, and I'm the only one in the world who wants it to be alive.''

''Eh!'' Dickon almost whispered, ''it is a queer, pretty place! It's like as if a body was in a dream. I never thought I'd see this place. Martha told me there was a garden as no one ever went inside. Us used to wonder what it was like.''

''Will there be roses?'' Mary whispered. ''Can you tell? I thought perhaps they were all dead.''

''Eh! No! Not them—not all of 'em! There's lots o' dead wood as ought to be cut out. An' there's a lot o' old wood, but it has made some new last year. This here's a new bit,'' and he touched a shoot which looked brownish green instead of hard, dry gray. ''There's a lot of work to do here!'' Dickon said, looking about quite exultantly.

"Will you come again and help me to do it?" Mary begged. "I'm sure I can help, too. I can dig and pull up weeds, and do whatever you tell me. Oh! do come, Dickon!"

"I'll come every day if tha' wants me, rain or shine," he answered stoutly. "It's th' best fun I ever had in my life—shut in here an' wakenin' up a garden."

"Dickon," Mary said, "you are as nice as Martha said you were. I like you."

Dickon sat up on his heels as Martha did when she was polishing the grate. He did look funny and delightful, Mary thought, with his round blue eyes and red cheeks and happy turned-up nose. Then Mary did a strange thing. She leaned forward and asked him a question she had never dreamed of asking any one before. And she tried to ask it in Yorkshire because that was his language.

"Does tha' like me?" she said.

"Eh!" he answered heartily, "that I does. I likes thee wonderful, an' so does th' robin, I do believe!"

And then they began to work harder than ever and more joyfully. Mary was startled and sorry when she heard the big clock in the courtyard strike the hour of her midday dinner.

"I shall have to go," she said mournfully. "Whatever happens, you—you never would tell?"

"If tha' was a missel thrush an' showed me where thy nest was, does tha' think I'd tell any one? Not me," he said. "Tha' art as safe as a missel thrush."

And she was quite sure she was.

Mary ate her dinner as quickly as she could and when she rose from the table she was going to run to her room to put on her hat again, but Martha stopped her.

"I've got somethin' to tell you," she said. "Mr. Craven came back this mornin' and I think he wants to see you. He's goin' for a long time. He mayn't come back till autumn or winter. He's goin' to travel in foreign places. He's always doin' it."

"Oh! I'm so glad—so glad!" said Mary thankfully.

If he did not come back until winter, there would be time to watch the secret garden come alive. Even if he found out then and took it away from her she would have had that much at least.

Mrs. Medlock took her to a part of the house she had not been into before. At last Mrs. Medlock knocked at a door, and when someone said, "Come in," they entered the room together. A man was sitting in an armchair before the fire. When Mrs. Medlock went out and closed the door, she could see that the man in the chair was a man with high, rather crooked shoulders, and he had black hair streaked with white. He was not ugly. His face would have been handsome if it had not been so miserable. His black eyes seemed as if they scarcely saw her.

"I forgot you," he said. "I intended to send you a governess or a nurse, but I forgot."

"Please," began Mary. "Please—I am too big for a nurse. I want to play out of doors. I never liked it in India. It makes me hungry here, and I am getting fatter."

"Mrs. Sowerby said it would do you good."

"Is she—is she Martha's mother?" she stammered.

"Yes, I think so," he replied. "She thought you had better get stronger before you had a governess."

"It makes me feel strong when I play and the wind comes over the moor," argued Mary. "I don't do any harm."

"You could not do any harm, a child like you! You may do what you like."

"May I?" she said tremulously.

"Of course you may. I wish you to be happy and comfortable. It's a big place and you may go where you like and amuse yourself as you like. Is there anything you want? Do you want toys, books, dolls?"

"Might I," quavered Mary, "might I have a bit of earth?"

Mr. Craven looked quite startled. "Earth! What do you mean?"

"To plant seeds in—to make things grow—to see them come alive," Mary faltered.

Mr. Craven got up and began to walk slowly across the room. When he stopped and spoke to her his dark eyes looked almost soft and kind.

"You remind me of some one else who loved the earth and things that grow. When you see a bit of earth you want, take it, child, and make it come alive."

"May I take it from anywhere—if it's not wanted?"

"Anywhere," he answered. "Goodbye. I shall be away all summer."

Mary flew back to her room. She found Martha waiting there.

"I can have my garden!" cried Mary. "He says a little girl like me could not do any harm and I may do what I like—anywhere!"

"Eh!" said Martha delightedly, "that was nice of him, wasn't it?"

That night Mary was awakened by the sound of rain beating against her window and the mournful sound of the "wuthering" wind. Suddenly something made her sit up in bed and turn her head toward the door listening.

"It isn't the wind now," she said in a loud whisper. "That isn't the wind. It is different. It is that crying I heard before."

The sound came down the corridor, a far-off faint sound of fretful crying.

"I am going to find out what it is," she said. "Everybody is in bed and I don't care about Mrs. Medlock—I don't care!"

There was a candle by her bedside and she took it up and went softly out of the room. The far-off faint crying went on and led her. Down this passage and then to the left, and then up two broad steps, and then to the right again. She could hear the crying quite plainly on the other side of the wall at her left and a few yards farther on there was a door. She could see a glimmer of light coming from beneath it. The Someone was crying in that room, and it was quite a young Someone.

So she walked to the door and pushed it open, and there she was standing in the room!

It was a big room with ancient, handsome furniture in it. There was a low fire glowing faintly on the hearth and a night light burning by the side of a carved four-poster bed hung with brocade, and on the bed was lying a boy, crying fretfully.

The boy had a sharp, delicate face the color of ivory and he seemed to have eyes too big for it. He looked like a boy who had been ill, but he was crying more as if he were tired and cross than as if he were in pain.

Mary crept across the room, and, as she drew nearer, the light attracted the boy's attention and he turned and stared at her, his gray eyes opening so wide that they seemed immense.

"Who are you?" he said at last in a half-frightened whisper. "Are you a ghost?"

"No, I am not," Mary answered. "Are you one?"

"No, I am Colin."

"Who is Colin?" she faltered.

"I am Colin Craven. Who are you?"

"I am Mary Lennox. Mr. Craven is my uncle."

"He is my father," said the boy.

"Your father!" gasped Mary. "No one ever told me he had a boy! What were you crying for?"

"Because I couldn't go to sleep and my head ached. I am like this always, ill and having to lie down. If I live I may be a hunchback, but I shan't live. My father hates to think I may be like him."

"Have you been here always?"

"Nearly always. Sometimes I have been taken to places at the seaside, but I won't stay because people stare at me. I used to wear an iron thing to keep my back straight. I hate fresh air and I don't want to go out. How old are you?" he asked.

"I am ten," answered Mary, "and so are you."

"How do you know that?" he demanded in a surprised voice.

"Because when you were born the garden door was locked and the key was buried. And it has been locked for ten years."

"What garden door was locked? Who did it? Where was the key buried?" he exclaimed as if he were suddenly very much interested. The idea of a garden attracted him as it had attracted her. He asked question after question. "I don't think I ever really wanted to see anything before, but I want to see that garden. I am going to make them open the door."

He had become quite excited and his strange eyes began to shine like stars. Mary's hands clutched each other. Everything would be spoiled! Dickon would never come back.

"Oh, don't—don't—don't do that!" she cried out.

"Why?" he exclaimed. "You said you wanted me to see it."

"I do, but if you make them open the door and take you in it will never be a secret again. Oh, don't you see how much nicer it would be if it was a secret?"

"I never had a secret," he said, "except that I might not live to grow up. They don't know I know that, so it is a sort of secret. But I like this kind better."

"If you won't make them take you to the garden," pleaded Mary, "I feel almost sure I can find out how to get in sometime."

"I should like that. I should not mind fresh air in a secret garden."

She leaned against the bed and began to stroke and pat his hand and sing a very low little chanting song in Hindustani.

"That is nice," he said drowsily, and when she looked at him again he was fast asleep. So she got up softly and crept away without making a sound.

The next day Mary and Colin both talked and listened as they had never done before. They enjoyed themselves so much that they forgot about the time. And in the midst of the fun the door opened and in walked Mrs. Medlock and Dr. Craven, who was both the local physician and Mr. Archibald Craven's closest living relative, except, of course, for Colin.

"Good Lord!" exclaimed poor Mrs. Medlock.

"What is this?" said Dr. Craven, coming forward. "What does it mean?"

"This is my cousin, Mary Lennox," Colin answered. "I like her. She must come and talk to me whenever I send for her."

Mary saw that Dr. Craven did not look pleased, but it was quite plain that he dare not oppose his patient.

"I am afraid there has been too much excitement. Excitement is not good for you, my boy," he said.

"I should be excited if she kept away," answered Colin, his eyes beginning to look dangerously sparkling. "She makes me better."

Dr. Craven did not look happy when he left the room. The boy actually did look brighter, however—and he sighed rather heavily as he went down the corridor.

In her talks with Colin, Mary tried to be very cautious about the secret garden. She wanted to discover whether he was the kind of boy you could tell a secret to.

"I was thinking," said Mary, "how different you are from Dickon."

"Who is Dickon?" said Colin.

"He is Martha's brother," she explained. "He can charm foxes and squirrels just as the natives in India charm snakes. He knows all about eggs and nests, and where badgers and otters live. He keeps them secret so that other boys won't find them."

Mary went on about Dickon's mother—and the skipping-rope—and the moor with the sun on it—and about pale green points sticking up out of the black sod. And it was all so alive that Mary talked more than she had ever talked before—and Colin both talked and listened as he had never done either before.

On the first sunny morning after a week of rain Mary wakened very early. She ran out to the secret garden where Dickon was already working hard.

"Oh, Dickon!" she cried out. "How could you get here so early! The sun has only just got up!"

"Eh!" he said, laughing and glowing. "I was up long before him. Th' world's all fair begun again this mornin', it has."

A little bushy-tailed animal rose from its place under a dwarf apple-tree and came to him, and a rook, cawing once, flew down from its branch and settled quietly on his shoulder.

"This is th' little fox cub," he said, rubbing the little animal's head. "It's named Captain. An' this here's Soot. Soot he flew across th' moor with me an' Captain."

"There is something I want to tell you," she whispered. "Do you know about Colin?"

"Everybody as knowed about Mester Craven knowed there was a little lad as was like to be a cripple, an' they knowed Mester Craven didn't like him to be talked about."

"Do you think he wants to die?" whispered Mary.

"No, but he wishes he'd never been born."

"He's been lying in his room so long that it has made him queer," said Mary. "But he likes to hear about this garden because it is a secret. I daren't tell him much but he said he wanted to see it."

"Us'll have him out here sometime for sure," said Dickon. "I could push his carriage well enough. Has tha' noticed how th' robin and his mate has been workin' while we've been sittin' here? Us is nest-buildin' too, bless thee," he said to the robin.

The garden had reached the time when every day it seemed as if magicians were passing through it drawing loveliness out of the earth and the boughs with wands. It was hard to go away and leave it all, but Mary went back to the house and sat down close to Colin's bed.

"Can I trust you? I trusted Dickon because birds trusted him. Can I trust you—*for sure?*" she implored.

"Yes—yes!"

"There is a door into the garden. I found it."

"Oh! Mary!" he cried out. "Shall I get to see it?" and he clutched her hands.

"Of course you'll see it!" snapped Mary indignantly. Mary hesitated about two minutes and then spoke the truth.

"I found the key and got in weeks ago. But I daren't tell you because I was so afraid I couldn't trust you—*for sure!*"

That night Colin slept without once awakening and when he opened his eyes in the morning he lay still and smiled. The next minute Mary was in the room and had run across to his bed, bringing with her a waft of fresh air full of the scent of the morning. They ate their breakfast with the morning air pouring in upon them. In about ten minutes Mary held up her hand.

"Listen!" she said. "Did you hear a caw?"

Colin listened and heard it, the oddest sound in the world to hear inside a house, a hoarse "caw-caw."

"If you please, sir," announced Martha, opening the door, "here's Dickon an' his creatures."

Dickon came in smiling his nicest wide smile. A new-born lamb was in his arms and the little red fox trotted by his side. A squirrel sat on his left shoulder and Soot on his right and another squirrel's head and paws peeped out of his coat pocket.

Colin slowly sat up and stared—a stare of wonder and delight. He had not understood what this boy would be like and that his fox and his crow and his squirrels and his lamb were so near to him that they seemed almost to be part of himself.

Dickon walked over to Colin's sofa and put the new-born lamb quietly on his lap, and the creature turned to the warm velvet dressing-gown and began to nuzzle into its folds.

"What is it doing?" cried Colin.

"It wants its mother," said Dickon, smiling. He knelt down and took a feeding-bottle from his pocket and pushed the rubber tip of the bottle into the nuzzling mouth.

Captain curled up near Dickon, who sat on the hearthrug. They

looked at the pictures in the gardening books and Dickon knew all the flowers by their country names and knew exactly which ones were already growing in the secret garden.

"I'm going to see them," cried Colin. "I am going to see them!"

"Aye, that tha' mun," said Mary quite seriously. "An' tha' munnot lose no time about it."

But they were obliged to wait more than a week because first there came some very windy days and then Colin was threatened with a cold. The most absorbing thing, however, was the preparations to be made before Colin could be transported with sufficient secrecy to the garden. No one must see the chair-carriage and Dickon and Mary after they turned a certain corner of the shrubbery and entered upon the walk outside the ivied walls.

The head gardener, Mr. Roach, was startled one day when he received orders from Master Colin's room to the effect that he must report himself in the apartment no outsider had ever seen, as the invalid himself desired to speak to him. When the bedroom door was opened, a large crow announced the entrance of a visitor by saying "Caw—Caw" quite loudly. Mr. Roach only just escaped being sufficiently undignified to jump backward.

Roach wondered if he was to receive instructions to fell all the oaks or to transform the orchards into water-gardens.

"Oh, you are Roach, are you?" Colin said. "I sent for you to give some very important orders. I am going out in my chair this afternoon. When I go, none of the gardeners are to be anywhere near the Long Walk by the garden walls. No one is to be there. I shall go out about two o'clock and everyone must keep away until I send word."

"Very good, sir," replied Mr. Roach, much relieved to hear that the oaks and the orchards were safe.

"You have my permission to go, Roach," Colin said. "But, remember, this is very important."

A little later the nurse made Colin ready. She noticed that, instead of lying like a log while his clothes were put on, he sat up and made some efforts to help himself. The strongest footman in the house carried Colin downstairs and put him in his wheeled chair, near which Dickon waited outside. After the manservant had arranged his rugs and cushions, Colin waved his hand to him and to the nurse and they both disappeared quickly.

Dickon began to push the wheeled chair slowly and steadily. Mistress Mary walked beside it and Colin leaned back and lifted his face to the sky. Not a human creature was to be caught sight of in the paths they took. In fact, every gardener or gardener's lad had been witched away. When at last they turned into the Long Walk by the ivied walls the excited sense of an approaching thrill made them begin to speak in whispers.

"This is where the robin flew over the wall," breathed Mary. "And that is where he perched on the little heap of earth and showed me the key. And this is the ivy the wind blew back," and she took hold of the hanging green curtain.

"Oh! is it—is it!" gasped Colin.

"And here is the handle, and here is the door. Dickon, push him in quickly!"

And Dickon did it with one strong, steady, splendid push.

But Colin had actually dropped back against his cushion and he had covered his eyes with his hands and held them there until they were inside and the chair stopped as if by magic and the door was closed. Not till then did he take them away and look round and round as Dickon and Mary had done. And over walls and earth and trees and swinging sprays and tendrils the fair green veil of tender little leaves had crept. And the sun fell warm upon his face like a hand with a lovely touch.

"I shall get well! I shall get well!" he cried out. "Mary! Dickon! I shall get well! And I shall live forever and ever and ever!"

That afternoon the whole world seemed to devote itself to being perfect and radiantly beautiful and kind to one boy. Perhaps out of pure heavenly goodness the spring came and crowded everything it possibly could into that one place. Dickon pushed the chair slowly round and round the garden, stopping every other moment to let him look at wonders springing out of the earth or trailing down from trees.

"I shall come back tomorrow," said Colin, "and the day after, and the day after, and the day after."

"You'll get plenty of fresh air, won't you?" said Mary.

"I'm going to get nothing else," he answered. "I've seen the spring now and I'm going to see the summer."

"That tha' will," said Dickon. "Us'll have thee walkin' about here an' diggin' same as other folk afore long."

"I'm going to walk to that tree," Colin said, pointing to one a few feet away from him. "When I want to sit down I will sit down, but not before."

He walked to the tree and though Dickon held his arm he was wonderfully steady.

"Everyone thought I was going to die," said Colin shortly. "I'm not!"

He was a very proud boy. Later, back at the house, he lay thinking for a while and then Mary saw his beautiful smile begin.

"I shall stop being queer," he said, "if I go every day to the garden. There is magic in there, good magic, you know, Mary. I am sure there is."

"So am I," said Mary.

"Even if it isn't real magic," Colin said, "we can pretend it is. *Something* is there—*something!*"

"It's magic," said Mary, "but not black. It's as white as snow."

They always called it magic and indeed it seemed like it in the months that followed—the wonderful months—the radiant months—the amazing ones. Oh! the things which happened in that garden! The seeds Dickon and Mary had planted grew as if fairies had tended them. Fair fresh leaves, and buds—tiny at first but swelling until they burst and uncurled into cups of scent delicately filling the garden air.

Colin saw it all, watching each change as it took place.

"Magic is always pushing and drawing," he said, "and making things out of nothing. Every morning and evening I am going to say, 'Magic is in me! Magic is making me well! I am going to be as strong as Dickon!' Being alive is the magic—being strong is the magic. The magic is in me. It is in me—it is in me. It's in every one of us. Magic! Magic! Come and help!"

And Mary, too, had been affected by all these changes. Mrs. Medlock even remarked to Dr. Craven, "She's begun to be downright pretty since she's lost her ugly little sour look. Her hair's grown thick and healthy-looking and she's got a bright color. The glummest, ill-natured little thing she used to be and now her and Master Colin laugh together like a pair of crazy young ones!"

While the secret garden was coming alive and two children were coming alive with it, there was a man wandering about certain faraway places in the Norwegian fjords and the mountains of Switzerland. A terrible sorrow had fallen upon him when he had been happy and he had let his soul fill itself with blackness and had refused obstinately to allow any light to pierce through. He had deserted his home and his duties. His name was Archibald Craven.

As the golden summer changed into the deep golden autumn, he went to the Lake of Como. Now and then he wondered vaguely about his boy and asked himself what he should feel when he went and stood by the carved four-poster bed again and looked down at the sharply chiseled ivory-white face.

One marvel of a day he had walked so far that when he returned the moon was high and full and all the world was purple shadow and silver. He felt a strange calmness stealing over him and it grew deeper and deeper until he fell asleep and began to dream. He thought that as he sat and breathed in the scent of the late roses and listened to the lapping of the water at his feet he heard a voice calling.

"Archie! Archie!" it said, and then again, sweeter and clearer than before, "Archie! Archie!"

"Lilias!" he answered. "Lilias! where are you?"

"In the garden," it came back like the sound from a golden flute. "In the garden!"

And then the dream ended. The next morning he received a letter from Yorkshire. It was from Dickon's mother, who had noticed the wonderful improvement in both Mary and Colin.

"Dear Sir:

I am Susan Sowerby that made bold to speak to you once on the moor. Please, sir, I would come home if I was you. I think you would be glad to come and—if you will excuse me, sir—I think your lady would ask you to come if she was here.

Your obedient servant,
Susan Sowerby."

In a few days he was in Yorkshire again. When he arrived at the Manor he went into the library and sent for Mrs. Medlock.

"How is Master Colin, Medlock?" he inquired.

"Well, sir," Mrs. Medlock answered, "he's—he's different, in a manner of speaking."

"Worse?" he suggested.

"Well, you see, sir," she tried to explain, "neither Dr. Craven, nor the nurse, nor me can exactly make him out."

"Has he become more—more peculiar?" her master asked, knitting his brows anxiously.

"That's it, sir. He's growing very peculiar—when you compare him with what he used to be."

"Where is Master Colin now?" Mr. Craven asked.

"In the garden, sir. He's always in the garden—though not a human creature is allowed to go near for fear they'll look at him."

"In the garden," he said, and after he had sent Mrs. Medlock away he stood and repeated it again and again. "In the garden!"

He turned and went out of the room. He felt as if he were being drawn back to the place he had so long forsaken, and he did not know why. He knew where the door was even though the ivy hung thick over it—but he did not know exactly where it lay—that buried key. So he stopped and stood still, looking about him.

The ivy hung thick over the door, the key was buried under the shrubs, no human being had passed that portal for ten lonely years—and yet inside the garden there were sounds. They were the sound of running, scuffling feet seeming to chase round and round under the trees, they were strange sounds of lowered, suppressed voices—exclamations and smothered joyous cries.

And then the moment came, the uncontrollable moment when the sounds forgot to hush themselves. The feet ran faster and faster—and the door in the wall was flung wide open, and a boy burst through it at full speed and, without seeing the outsider, dashed almost into his arms.

Mr. Craven had extended them just in time to save him from falling as a result of his unseeing dash against him, and when he held him away to look at him in amazement at his being there, he truly gasped for breath.

He was a tall boy and a handsome one. He was glowing with life. He threw the thick hair back from his forehead and lifted a pair of strange gray eyes.

"Who—What? Who?" he stammered.

This was not what Colin had expected—this was not what he had planned. He had never thought of such a meeting. And yet to come dashing out—winning a race—perhaps it was even better. He drew himself up to his very tallest.

"Father," he said, "I'm Colin. You can't believe it. I scarcely can myself. I'm Colin."

He said it all so like a healthy boy that Mr. Craven's soul shook with unbelieving joy.

"Aren't you glad, Father?" he ended. "Aren't you glad? I'm going to live forever and ever!"

Mr. Craven put his hands on both the boy's shoulders and held him still.

"Take me into the garden, my boy," he said. "And tell me about it."

And so they led him in. Late roses climbed and hung and clustered and the sunshine deepening the hue of the yellowing trees made one feel that one stood in an embowered temple of gold.

"I thought it would be dead," he said.

"Mary thought so at first," said Colin. "But it came alive. Now it need not be a secret any more. I dare say it will frighten them nearly into fits when they see me. I shall walk back with you, Father—to the house."

When Mrs. Medlock looked out the window she threw up her hands and gave a little shriek and every man and woman servant within hearing bolted across the servants' hall and stood looking through the window with their eyes almost staring out of their heads.

Across the lawn came the Master of Misselthwaite and he looked as many of them had never seen him. And by his side with his head up in the air and his eyes full of laughter walked as strongly and steadily as any boy in Yorkshire—Master Colin!

THE END